DO YOU ENJOY BEING FRIGHTENED?

**WOULD YOU RATHER HAVE
NIGHTMARES
INSTEAD OF SWEET DREAMS?**

**ARE YOU HAPPY ONLY WHEN
SHAKING WITH FEAR?**

CONGRATULATIONS ! ! ! !

Y

T

TO

2-21-13
8.19.19

RUN   E!

Shivers ™

BABYFACE AND

To Jack and Sondra
and
Bill and Lynne

Published by Paradise Press, Inc. by arrangement with River Publishing, Inc. All right, title and interest to the "SHIVERS" logo and design are owned by River Publishing, Inc. No portion of the "SHIVERS" logo and design may be reproduced in part or whole without prior written permission from River Publishing, Inc. An application for a registered trademark of the "SHIVERS" logo and design is pending with the Federal Patent and Trademark office.

ISBN 1-57657-092-4

EXCLUSIVE DISTRIBUTION BY PARADISE PRESS, INC.

Cover Design by George Paturzo
Cover Illustration by Eddie Roseboom

30621

Chapter One

I hate being a kid!

Ya know what I mean?

It's the worst.

All the dopey grown-ups in the world think they can push us around, just because we're smaller than they are.

They tell us all the time that we have to do stuff we don't want to do — or that we can't do stuff we really want to do.

And they're always giving us their stupid advice.

They act like we're dumb or something, just because we're only kids!

Don't ya just hate it?

I do!

Who are these people anyway to tell us how to behave, when to talk, where to sit? That kind of stuff is bad enough coming from our parents, ya know?

But when the orders come from other people — aunts, uncles, family friends — it just makes me crazy. Even strangers feel free to boss kids around.

I think it stinks! I say kids have got rights, too!

Why *shouldn't* we have rights?

Hey, plenty of kids are pretty smart — and some of us are a lot smarter than most adults.

Just being bigger doesn't make people any brighter, that's what I always say.

You're either intelligent or ya ain't — uh, I mean, *aren't*.

Ya either know your way around or ya don't. It's just that simple.

Well, let me tell ya pal, I *am* brighter than lots of adults. Honest I am.

And I really know my way around, too.

I'm a city kid, born and bred in a small apartment house near downtown Miami. Sure, I know you've heard about Miami so I won't bore you with all the details.

But if some adult was reading this book to you, he'd probably just have to tell you right now, "Miami's in Florida! It's a big city in the tropical part of the United States where palm trees are common." Like you don't already know that yourself, right?

Geez! Adults!

They're always trying to make themselves feel important or smart or whatever. And always at our expense!

Anyway, like I was saying, I'm a city kid. My name's Joey.

If you were right here next to me, I'd shake your hand. Pleased to meet ya, pal!

I'm a pretty friendly guy when it comes down to it. It's just that I get so angry when grown-ups treat me like I'm some little jerk.

I want to kick them in the shins or something

and yell, "Hey, buddy! Who died and left *you* in charge around here?"

Ya know what I mean?

It seems like most adults think that no one knows anything until he's at least twenty years old, and usually a lot older than that. I'm only thirteen now.

Sometimes I feel like I might burst if I have to wait another seven years to become a real adult. I'm just not sure I can stand to be a kid for that much longer!

I want to be free now — free of this endless childhood.

I want to be treated with respect, like I'm somebody important.

I want to be an adult!

But not just any adult. Nope, not me. Not old Joey.

I don't want to be a salesman or a fireman or even a baseball player.

I want to grow up to be a gangster!

A Mafia guy, just like in the movies.

Isn't that the coolest thing?

Call it whatever you want — gangster, mobster or just plain crook. That's my goal in life.

See, I'm growing up in kind of a rough neighborhood around Miami. That's what everyone says anyway.

I hang around guys who think they're pretty tough — and some of them *are* pretty tough, too!

They're gangsters. Real gangsters.

Wow! Now *that's* a great job.

But ya have to make it into a really good, really tough mob, see? Then you work your way up the ladder, until you run the show yourself. That's when you get to be the head boss, the top dog, the big banana.

Someday that's gonna be me.

If I ever grow up, that is!

I've pleaded with some of the local mobsters to take me into their gang, but they always say, "You're too young, punk! Go play with your dolls!"

Or something just as stupid as that.

The jerks!

Geez!

I just want to prove that I can handle it. That's all I want — a chance!

I have to admit, I'm not too sure exactly what real gangsters do all day long. It seems like they mostly hang out with each other and talk really tough.

That's the coolest part of the job, I think.

Remember, I said that I'm a pretty friendly guy. I'd enjoy standing around and talking with the other guys in the gang all day long, bragging about all the tough things we're gonna do.

To tell you the truth, though, I don't enjoy violence much. It's not like I really want to hurt nobody — uh, I mean, *anybody*.

I'm not too crazy about that part of the job, I guess.

But hey, don't get me wrong. I'm no sissy, either!

I can fight better than most guys if I have to. I'm plenty tough.

So if the mob boss needs old Joey to punch out some bad guy for him, I can do that.

Or if he needs me to steal something from another gang for him, no problem for old Joey!

Or if he needs me to collect all the cash from his gambling joints, Joey can do that too.

Sure, I could — if someone would ever let me try.

But at this rate, I'll be old and gray before I ever get a shot at joining a real Mafia gang.

So here I am, thinking like this for weeks and months. Even years, it seems like.

Every day, I'm thinking this same stuff, over and over, wanting really bad to grow up and join the gang.

Then one afternoon I'm kind of just walking down the street, around the corner from my house, see? I'm sort of feeling low and angry because I'm still just a kid.

And that's when it happens to me.

Chapter Two

All of a sudden, a bunch of the local mob guys come storming down the street. Five of them, all walking as fast as they can walk. Almost running.

They're members of the Killer Mob, the biggest and meanest gang in Miami. The gang I want to join.

They're carrying baseball bats and tire irons, knives and guns. And they look plenty angry.

And they're walking right toward me, staring me in the eye!

Right away I start thinking: Hey, I'm in big trouble here! Lou and Rocco and Jimmy and Jackie and Mikey look like they want to kill me or something!

And then I begin wondering: What have I

done to make them so mad at me? Well, who knows but I'd better get the heck out of here!

So I'm ready to run for my life like a frightened dog!

But just as I take the first step, I notice they're not really looking at me — they're looking over my head.

They're walking toward some house down the street, probably planning to beat up some other tough guy who lives there.

Maybe it's the house of another mobster who didn't pay back a loan or something. Whatever.

And now I'm thinking: Hey, maybe this is my chance.

So I start begging the guys in the mob: "Hey Rocco! Yo, Jimmy! How ya doing? Take me with you guys, will ya?"

"Get lost!" Jimmy says.

"Yeah, beat it, twerp!" Rocco says.

"Come on, boys! I can help ya out!" I holler.

That's when Jackie comes over to me, looking really serious about everything. Jackie never smiles anyway. He's really tough, kind of an assistant to the top boss.

"Here, kid! You're always trying to join the gang," Jackie says. "Take this and come with us, if you want in our mob so bad!"

And Jackie reaches inside his coat pocket and pulls out a small silver gun!

I can tell by the way he's handling it that the gun is loaded.

"Go ahead kid, take it!" Jackie orders, shoving the gun into my hand. I have to admit my hand is starting to shake a little now. I've never held a real gun before. "We've got to bump somebody off. Ya know, kill 'em! So we'll let you do the killing for us! OK, kid? And if you do it right, you're in the mob, right boys?"

"Yeah, that's right, Jackie! Sure," Rocco agrees.

"Yeah, why not?" Lou says.

"But ya got to get up real close to him, and

stick the gun to his head and . . . " Jackie says.

"I — I can't, uh, do that!" I hear myself saying. "I d-don't want to kill nobody!"

"Listen, kid! Ya wanted in the gang. Now you're in — and you're gonna do what we tell ya to do. *Or else*," Jackie says angrily. "Now get going!"

"Uh, or else — what?" I gulp nervously.

"Or else, we'll kill *you*!" Jackie yells.

And three of the guys push me ahead of them.

Whether I want it or not, I'm in the gang now.

Sure, I was all hot to join the mob. But not like this!

Suddenly, I have to become a killer — a hard, cold, tough, brutal, mob murderer!

Me! Old Joey!

And I know I'd better do it, too — no matter how much I don't want to!

Or the mob is gonna murder me instead!

<u>Chapter Three</u>

So now I'm walking along in front of the gang, see? And I'm thinking to myself: OK, smart boy! *Now* what are ya gonna do?

I mean, there's no way I'm going to be able to pull the trigger and really shoot somebody, ya know? It's too awful to even think about.

But if I *don't* do that, I'd better find some way out of this fix — really fast! Or I won't live long enough to grow up.

Maybe I could outrun the boys! Yeah, maybe. But then I couldn't ever come back to my apartment because the mob would be hunting for me everywhere, trying to rub me out.

And they might even hurt my parents or something.

Nah, that's no good, I'm thinking, desperate for a better idea.

OK, so maybe I can talk my way out of this thing somehow. I could tell the guys that I want to be in the gang all right, sure. But for something this big, well, I ain't quite ready — uh, I mean, I'm *not* quite ready.

Yeah, that's the trick, sure, I decide. Talk your way out, Joey.

So I begin to explain as we're walking along. But the guys aren't buying any of it, ya know?

"So, Jackie, I'm not sure I know how to use this kind of gun," I say nervously. "This isn't the kind of gun I'm used to. So maybe you should do this job and let me watch. OK? Then next time, I can do it. Yeah, that's probably a better way to handle this job, don't ya think?"

"Listen, kid. A gun's a gun! You aim the barrel and pull the trigger and that's it," Jackie says, like he's really ticked off at me. "If ya can shoot one gun, ya can shoot any of 'em!"

"What's the matter, kid? Getting cold feet?" Rocco asks. "Ain't ya never killed no one before?"

"Sure I have!" I lie. "Lots of times. Hey, I ain't no pansy, ya know!"

"Good, 'cause here's your chance, kid," Lou says. "This is the bum's house. The boss wants us to rub him out 'cause he's not paying the money he owes us, see? Now go knock on the door and do it, kid. Now!"

So I'm really in the middle of a terrible jam this time, ya know what I mean?

And I know lying didn't work so maybe I'm gonna have to tell the guys the truth, like it or not. It might be the best chance I have to get out of this mess with my life.

"OK, guys, see — this is the deal. I haven't really shot a gun before, and that's the real truth," I start explaining. "And I sure haven't ever shot anybody. And to be real honest, I don't ever want to shoot anyone, ya know? I don't like blood so much."

"Oh yeah? Well, we thought you wanted in

the mob so bad," Jimmy says. "But I guess you can't handle it after all, tough guy! So maybe we're gonna have to take the gun back from you, huh?"

"Yeah, and then shoot you!" Jackie says, grabbing the gun from my hand.

"Wait, Jackie! Don't shoot me!" I start screaming. "I don't deserve it."

"Sure ya do, kid. Ya chickened out on your gang," Jackie says, pointing the gun at me. "And for that, ya have to die!"

And now I know for sure he's going to pull the trigger and that's it, boy! I'm a goner for sure.

Chapter Four

I turn away so I won't have to look. But Jackie spins me around to face him, and he sticks the barrel of the gun against my forehead. I can feel myself ready to cry, I'm so scared!

I'm just waiting to hear the bang and drop dead on the ground.

But instead of a bang I hear something else — kind of like water trickling.

And then I feel my forehead's getting real wet and something is running down my face — something cold and wet, and I know it's not blood.

That's when I finally get it. The gun is really only a water pistol!

Real funny, huh? Big men, scaring a little kid to death like that!

All five of these thugs are bursting out laughing now. They're practically rolling on the ground and they're slapping their legs. Tears start coming down their cheeks from laughing so hard.

"Kid, I thought you was gonna have a heart attack or something," Jimmy says, snorting through his nose as he laughs.

"So you're a big mobster, huh, kid? Yeah, you're ready to join the gang," Jackie says, laughing. "Maybe in about twenty years!"

"Yeah, you ain't nothing but a pansy, kid. Maybe we should call you Joanne instead of Joey," Rocco chuckles.

It turns out the guys aren't planning to rub out anyone on this street at all. The whole thing is their idea of a gag. They did all this as a practical joke, just to bug me because they know how bad I want to join up with their mob.

So now I start complaining, getting really angry with them.

"You guys are such a bunch of jerks!" I yell.

"Don't ever pull something like that on me again or I'll get all of you!"

"Yeah, you and what army?" Rocco answers, laughing.

"I won't need an army, see? Because I know where all you punks live," I say. "I'll just walk over to Biscayne Boulevard and talk with Tony and the Muscle Gang. And I'll tell them where you guys live so they can knock off all five of you!"

The Muscle Gang is the second-biggest mob in Miami, the toughest rival of the Killer Mob. Tony is the leader of the Muscle Gang.

I know how much Jackie and Rocco and Jimmy and Lou and Mikey hate the Muscle Gang. And I also know how much they worry that someone from the Muscle Gang will come along and hurt them someday.

So that's why I'm threatening to rat on them to the Muscle Gang. Even though I wouldn't ever really do that, see?

But now I'm starting to think maybe this

wasn't such a smart thing to say. Because all five guys are staring at me, looking really angry. And they're also looking like they want to shoot me for real this time.

"What did you say?" Mikey asks with a menacing tone. Mikey doesn't talk much — and when he does, it's always bad. "You gonna rat on us, kid? That what you said? Hey Jackie, I say we kill the kid first, before he can talk to the Muscle Gang."

"Yeah, I've had enough of this little punk, Jackie," Rocco says. "Let me throw him in the river!"

"Yeah, if he's gonna rat, we need to knock him off. Right now!" Lou agrees.

So I'm getting really scared. I mean *really* scared!

Ya know what I'm saying?

Think how you'd feel right about now. You've got five thugs all snarling and cursing at you. And some of them are just begging to throw you in the Miami River!

You know that if they throw you in, you'll be

wearing cement shoes and you will sink right to the bottom of the river and drown.

"No, Jackie! Wait!" I say. "I was just kidding with you guys! Ya know me. Little old Joey! I wouldn't hurt a fly. And besides, I want to join your gang. I wouldn't hurt you guys!"

"Then ya shouldn't have said nothing about ratting on us, kid!" Jackie sneers. "Because in our business, we can't take chances!"

"No Jackie! Please!" I say. "Please, listen to me, will ya? I didn't mean it, honest! I was just joking back, 'cause you guys played a rotten trick on me. That's all it was. Honest, Jackie! Can't you guys take a joke?"

But Jackie isn't in any mood for jokes — at least, not jokes about the Muscle Gang. He's mad. And this time, I can tell for sure that he's not playing a gag on me.

Jackie is gritting his teeth, like a rabid dog that's ready to bite.

"Grab the kid, Mikey!" he orders. "Take him

to the river and push him in! And make sure he don't come back up again! Make sure the kid keeps his big mouth shut — forever!"

Chapter Five

I'm in big, big trouble for real this time!

And this ain't no mob joke! Uh, I mean, *isn't* any mob joke.

Mobsters are in a very dangerous business. And if some guy like me threatens to make the danger any worse than it already is, he probably won't live long.

I should have known that. But I guess I got so angry that I forgot.

So now, Mikey picks me up by the waist, with one hand over my mouth so I can't scream or anything.

"Where do you want I should dump him, Jackie?" Mikey asks.

"You said you was gonna drop him in the

river. That's good enough," Jackie answers. "They'll never look for him there. Just make sure he don't come floating back up, ya know?"

"Sure, sure, I know what ya mean," Mikey says. "Ain't I done this same thing a hundred times before? I know the routine. I'll use some good cement, Jackie. I'll make sure this kid stays at the bottom for a long time."

I'm more scared than I've ever been in my life! I don't want to end up at the bottom of the river!

What am I gonna do, I keep wondering. How can I get away?

I try to scream but Mikey's holding my mouth shut and I can't make a peep. I struggle to get away but Mikey's got big, strong hands and he just squeezes me tighter than ever.

No way! I'm stuck — and as good as dead!

So while Mikey holds on to me, Rocco goes for his car and then the two of them stuff me in the back seat. Rocco drives and Mikey sits in the back with me.

"You shut up, kid! Ya hear me?" Mikey says. "If you scream, I'll blow you away right here in the car!"

I can tell by his face that Mikey means every word. So I just sit real quiet, thinking like crazy, my brain moving at a hundred miles an hour.

I'm thinking, maybe when Mikey opens the door, I can make a run for it!

And I'm thinking, maybe I can grab Mikey's gun somehow and use it to get away!

And I'm thinking, maybe before the cement hardens around my feet, I can grab a handful of it and throw cement in Mikey's and Rocco's eyes! Then I can head for some place to hide out!

I know there isn't much hope any of these tricks will really work. But I'm not giving up, no matter how bleak and frightening everything seems.

Hey, why should I give up?

I still have some chance to escape — *if* I can think of something smart enough to fool these thugs.

The car moves on through the hot Miami streets, and even though Rocco has the air conditioning on, I'm sweating a lot. I know I may not have much time left to live.

We pull into a little side street somewhere. I haven't been around here before so I have no idea where we are.

There are lots of steel warehouses on both sides of the street, and it looks like kind of a dumpy, rundown area. We drive for what seems like blocks and blocks and then the car comes to a stop.

I gulp. I still don't have a good plan to make my getaway.

But I know I'd better try something!

Looking around for cops, Rocco gets out of the car. He has his gun drawn, and pointed right at me. Mikey opens the door and gives me a push.

"OK, kid! Get out!" Mikey growls.

"Yeah, sure, Mikey. Anything you say," I answer. "But listen, guys! Honest! I was just kidding with you about the Muscle Gang! I wouldn't rat on anyone in the Killer Mob! Never ever! Please believe me!"

"Well, then, think of this as your first lesson about being in a gang," Rocco replies. "Ya don't ever joke around about ratting on your pals, see?"

"Yeah, this is kind of your first lesson about the mob — and your *last* one, too," Mikey says with a mean laugh. "Too bad ya won't never get to grow up and be in the gang with us, kid!"

So now Mikey grabs me by the shoulders and pushes me over toward a warehouse door. And when Rocco unlocks that door and opens it, I see something inside that makes my stomach sink and my skin crawl.

I see a big metal bucket and beside it, two large sacks made of thick brown paper. And each sack has the same word written on it: "CEMENT."

They really are going to put my feet in cement and throw me in the Miami River!

__Chapter Six__

Without thinking, I turn and bolt desperately for the street.

But I'm not quick enough — Mikey just grabs my shirt collar and yanks me back to him.

"Don't try nothing smart, kid! Ya ain't getting away from us, so ya can just forget it!" he says.

Out of nowhere, another car screeches around the corner and roars down the street toward the warehouse. It's a big black car racing at top speed.

Suddenly, Mikey lets me go.

He and Rocco dive inside the warehouse, pulling out their guns as the car screams closer and closer.

That's when I finally figure out what's going

on.

It's the Muscle Gang!

This black car is full of members of the Muscle Gang, a hit squad trying to knock off Mikey and Rocco.

And me!

I'm caught right in the middle of a battle between the Muscle Gang and the Killer Mob!

As bullets start to fly all around me, whizzing past my ears from the front and from the back, I realize that I'm standing in the worst possible place!

Out in the open, with no place to take cover!

And I also realize that, any moment now, I'm going to get a bullet in my chest from the Muscle Gang. Or a bullet in my back from the Killer Mob!

Or both!

Chapter Seven

Kaaa-paaap! Kaaa-paaap!
Bullets whiz all around me.
Kaaa-paaap! Kaaa-paaap! Kaaa-paaap! Kaaa-paaap!

The Muscle Gang's car is stopped in front of the warehouse, doors open, five men crawling out to fire their pistols and rifles.

Rocco and Mikey are lying on the warehouse floor, firing wildly at their attackers, loading and re-loading their guns.

I'm lying down, too. In the middle of the street, hands over my head.

Kaaa-paaap! Kaaa-paaap! Kaaa-paaap! Kaaa-paaap!

Gunfire cracks around me like thunderclaps,

blue smoke filling the air.

And I understand I'd better get out of here right away, or I may never leave at all!

But where can I go?

In front of me is the Muscle Gang — and I know they would only shoot me if I crawled to their car.

After all, they found me at the warehouse with the Killer Mob.

Behind me is the Killer Mob — and I know Rocco and Mikey would only shoot me if I crawled back to the warehouse.

After all, they think I'm going to rat on them to the Muscle Gang.

It looks hopeless! Totally, terribly hopeless!

I'm pinned down by the barrage of bullets, a barrage that sometimes misses me by only an inch or two.

The Muscle Gang begins to spread out now, firing their guns and then running and rolling from one trash can to the next, or from one parked car to another along the little street. They take cover wherever they can find it.

And with each step they make, all five gangsters move nearer and nearer to the warehouse.

As the attackers close in, Mikey and Rocco edge deeper and deeper inside the warehouse. They know that they're outnumbered, that they're both goners unless they can stay hidden from the assault.

Without warning, the Muscle Gang jumps up and dashes toward the warehouse, their guns blazing madly! All five of them rush Rocco and Mikey in a crazy do-or-die charge!

That's when I know it's time to make my move.

It's now or never, I think.

With all the gunplay back and forth, no one notices me scrambling to my feet — and starting to run away from the battle with all my strength!

I may as well tell you that I'm no bigger than most kids my age, no taller or heavier. I'm not really the brawny type either, with lots of muscles or anything.

But I'm tough enough and strong enough when I need to be.

And I need to be now!

So I'm tearing down the street at top speed, my feet flying like an Olympic sprinter or something.

I'm doing it!

I'm getting away!

I'm going to live!

Behind me, I can hear the gunfight getting worse and worse, a flurry of shots that sounds like some kind of war.

It must be pretty ugly back there now, I think. Then, just for an instant, I wonder, if I should go back and help Rocco and Mikey.

Maybe I should try to do something, I think.

But as I turn my head to look back toward the warehouse, I slip on a patch of slick oil in the street. I totally lose my footing!

And I go down like a rock!

Fwaap!

I feel my head slam into the pavement as hard as any hammer ever hit a nail.

For a minute, I get really confused, I guess.

Really, really, really confused!

I mean, it's almost like I'm not sure where I am — or even *who* I am! Or anything else.

Everything seems real foggy and dim around me, as if smoke from the mobsters' guns is swirling around my head, choking me.

I feel kind of sick, too. And for just a second, I'm afraid I'll throw up right here — wherever "here" is!

All of a sudden, everything seems even weirder than I thought it was!

Because somehow I'm inside Rocco's car, see?

Only I'm *driving* the thing, if you can believe it!

No fooling, pal! I'm actually behind the wheel of this gangster's car!

And I'm thinking: Wow! What's happening

here? Is this strange or what?

But I don't have any time to figure it out.

Because this car is moving — really fast!

It's flying at a speed that feels like at least a hundred and twenty miles an hour!

And there's no one in this car but me! Yeah, I'm actually driving the car right into the thick of the awful gun battle between the Muscle Gang and the Killer Mob!

As if that isn't bad enough, I know there's something even more terrifying about this bizarre situation.

Something I suddenly remember in a panic as I yank at the wheel and the buildings race by me on either side.

I can't drive!

Chapter Eight

The car speeds totally out of control!

I want to scream for help — but for some reason, I don't.

As the car careens wildly toward the warehouse, it begins to swerve left and right, left and right, back and forth across the street.

I feel like the thing might tip over!

But the swerving does one *good* thing, too: The Muscle Gang is forced to scatter in different directions, running for their lives to avoid the speeding car.

A couple of the gang members fire shots toward me as the car races onward, but the bullets miss.

Somehow, I find the brake pedal and the car

squeals to a tire-smoking stop. I don't even know how I did it.

Rocco and Mikey fire off a couple of quick shots toward the Muscle Gang, then throw open the back door of the car and leap inside.

"Great work, Babyface!" Rocco says, puffing hard from fatigue and fear.

"Yeah, you was terrific to come rescue us like this, kid!" Mikey agrees, slamming shut the car door. "Let's get out of here!"

But I'm just thinking to myself: Sure, get out of here, huh? How am I gonna manage *that* one, buddy? I don't even know how to steer a car in a straight line!

And what does Rocco mean by calling me "Babyface" anyway?

One thing I found out real fast in Rocco's car: Driving is a lot trickier than it looks, ya know what I mean? I always thought it would be so easy.

But it ain't — uh, I mean, it *isn't*.

Then I look down toward the floor of the car.

And that's when I become aware of the strangest thing about this whole situation, something even stranger than finding myself behind the wheel of Rocco's car.

I discover that I can easily reach the gas and brake pedals while I'm sitting in the driver's seat.

How can that be, I wonder. Whenever my dad lets me sit in his driver's seat, my feet don't even come *close* to the pedals.

So then I glance at myself in the car's rear-view mirror — and I see I'm all grown up! Yeah, I'm not a kid any longer!

I'm inside an adult body now, with long legs and long arms and a big head and a big chest and everything. I even have a little stubble on my chin where I must have shaved off my whiskers that morning, though I suppose my face still looks pretty young.

Wow, talk about being weirded out!

In one bizarre instant, I've turned into a fully grown man! A mobster, just like I always wanted!

And I guess my name is Babyface now.

But I still can't seem to figure out how to drive the car. It's like my body suddenly grew up but my mind stayed the same as when I was thirteen years old.

"Uh, yeah, sure boys," I say to Rocco and Mikey, stalling for time. "Let's, uh, get out of here. As soon as I can get this darned . . . "

I start fiddling with the car's pedals as if something's wrong.

"Hey, what are ya doing, Babyface?" Rocco cries. "Get this thing in gear and take us to the boss!"

"Yeah, come on, kid! They're coming for us!" Mikey yells, firing three or four bullets out the car window toward the Muscle Gang.

I can see the five rival gangsters moving closer to the car, ducking and dodging and diving behind anything that can hide them from Rocco and Mikey.

Now and then, one of the guys from the Muscle Gang fires a bullet at the car.

"Hey, this ain't funny!" Mikey hollers, shooting out the window again.

"Yeah, step on it! Right now!" Rocco orders. "They're gonna surround the car and murder us all!"

"Well, sure, g-guys. Uh, except there's a little p-problem, I think," I stammer.

I realize we can't sit here all day or the Muscle Gang is gonna knock us off for sure. And I'm feeling real desperate.

How did I get to be an adult without learning to drive a car, I'm wondering. Well, I tell myself, I'd better figure it out pretty darned quick! Just do *something*!

So I decide to step on the gas pedal really hard, but when I do the car lurches forward violently.

And it stalls out!

The engine just stops running!

Remember, I've never started an automobile engine in my life so I don't know what to do next. I'm totally stumped here.

And the Muscle Gang is starting to come

nearer and nearer, shooting at our car more often. Rocco and Mikey return fire — and now they're getting really steamed at me.

"Hey, what is this!" Mikey shouts. "Some kind of set-up? You working for the Muscle Gang now or what, Babyface?"

"Start this car and drive out of here! *Now*!" Rocco screams. "We ain't got time to play any more games, kid!"

"Well, yeah, I want to start it, Rocco," I say. "But see, the problem is that . . . "

"I don't care *what* the problem is, Babyface!" Rocco interrupts, blasting his gun out the car window. Then he shoves the hot metal barrel of the gun against the back of my head. "You figure the problem out quick, kid! And get us out of here!"

"I'm *trying*, Rocco!" I shout fearfully. I feel like I want to cry or something, though I don't let myself shed a single tear. "It's just that I can't get the car started!"

"*You start this car and drive, Babyface*! I'll

give ya till the count of three!" Rocco bellows. "And if we ain't moving then, I'll blow your brains out, see?"

Chapter Nine

"One!" Rocco yells.

Now I can't think at all! I'm so afraid and so confused that my brain just won't work.

I need to make some decision fast — but I can't!

"*Two!*" Rocco shouts, pressing the gun harder against my head.

I can't move. I can't even speak!

I can't even begin to tell Rocco that I'm not with the Muscle Gang. It's only that I'm really a kid and I can't drive!

I've got my eyes closed, and I'm waiting for him to pull the trigger. But then, without warning, the Muscle Gang charges again!

Guns blaze all around me. Bullets break the

windshield and zing through the open window.

And all this chaos forces me to remember something that I'd seen Dad do a thousand times: turn the car key!

So at last I turn the key and the engine starts and I step on the gas pedal as hard as I can.

This time the car roars ahead, flying down the street as Rocco and Mikey shoot back toward the Muscle Gang. I glance in the rear-view mirror just long enough to see that no one was shot, despite the furious exchange of bullets.

Fortunately, Rocco and Mikey are safe. And I'm relieved to see all five guys from the Muscle Gang are standing around as if they're OK, too.

It's good that everyone from these two gangs was a bad shot, I think. Someone could really get hurt with all those guns going off!

Geez! Adults!

But now I remember that, hey, I'm an adult too.

At least, I sure look like an adult.

And I also remember that I still don't know how to drive a car!

Even though I'm doing it. Sort of!

The car is swinging here and there, back and forth across the road again. And the speedometer is climbing fast.

Sixty miles an hour!

Seventy miles an hour!

Eighty miles an hour!

Ninety miles an hour!

What should I do?

As they watch the Muscle Gang fade into the distance, Rocco and Mikey are too busy talking to notice how badly I'm driving.

"Man, we got out of there just in time, eh?" Mikey snarls to Rocco. And he starts reloading his gun.

"Yeah, what was with ya back there, Baby-face?" Rocco growls at me. "What was you thinking, waiting so long to hit the gas pedal? We thought ya was trying to get us killed or something."

Then Rocco and Mikey finally notice my horrible driving — and in the rear-view mirror, I see their eyes get wide with total fear!

"Hey, what's with you, kid?" Mikey shouts, clutching the back seat. "Ya gone nuts or something?"

"Geez, Babyface! You really *are* trying to kill us, ain't ya?" Rocco hollers. "Slow down! Slow down, will ya? You're crazy!"

By now, the speedometer reads nearly one hundred and twenty miles an hour!

We're moving at warp speed down the tiny side street. The warehouses that line our route are nothing but a blur.

We speed by a group of slow-moving cars faster than a 747 jet passes a flock of seagulls.

And we run through one stop sign after another as I pray that no other cars will roll across our path.

"Slow down, kid!" Mikey screams. "We've already left the Muscle Gang back there in our dust!"

"Hit the brakes, will ya, Babyface!" Rocco yells. "*Hit the brakes*!"

And so that's just what I do: hit the brakes. Hard.

Too hard!

The car begins to fishtail, the rear end swaying right and left. We're skidding as if I had tried to stop a speeding automobile on sheer ice, totally out of control.

And now the car is barreling toward a major intersection in downtown Miami, a corner where a traffic light tells motorists to stop and go. But the problem is that the light facing our car is red.

Red!

And I can't possibly stop!

We're heading right toward the side of a huge garbage truck that's rumbling through the intersection!

I let go of the steering wheel, cover my face and scream: *Aaaaaagggghhh*!

Rocco and Mikey cover their faces and

scream, too: *Aaaaaagggghhh*! *Aaaaaagggghhh*!

We're lucky about one thing. The truck driver sees us and moves out of the way just in time.

But our car slides sideways on screeching tires — and then starts to tumble and roll!

It slams into the street, end over end, the hood hitting, followed by the top, followed by the trunk, followed by the bottom and then the hood again!

Over and over, the car turns!

We're in one of the worst car crashes you can imagine, a total smash-up!

And not one of us from the Killer Mob is even wearing his seat belt!

Chapter Ten

The sound of metal crunching and glass crashing mixes with our screams!

It makes a terrible, spine-chilling noise.

Finally, the automobile flips on its top one last time, then stops with a groan. The whole car is giving off a heavy blue smoke that smells as sour as month-old milk.

And I start to move and whimper a little from all my bruises and small cuts. But now I realize that I'm pretty much OK, ya know?

It almost seems like some kind of miracle, but I actually survived the awful car wreck.

And so did Rocco and Mikey.

They're both just waking up after being knocked cold by the impact. They start moaning and coughing and everything.

Oooohhh! *Whhhheeeew*! *Kwaaaaacchh*!

Paaaaauuupp!

"Whoa! Wh-what happened?" Mikey says, his voice soft and groggy.

"Man! I — *Kwaaaaacchh*! *Paaaaauuupp*! — I don't know," Rocco answers, his voice confused and just as groggy.

"Are you guys OK?" I ask, turning around to look at my fellow gangsters. "We were in a crash. You're not hurt at all, are ya?"

"No, I guess we're . . . " Rocco begins.

Then suddenly he remembers what happened and looks really angry.

"Hey, that's right! This maniac almost got us killed, Mikey! What the heck was you thinking anyway, driving a hundred and twenty miles an hour down that little street?"

"Yeah, did you go completely nuts or wacko or something on us? Or what?" Mikey wonders, brushing the broken glass off his jacket.

"You must be crazy, Babyface! Driving like that!" Rocco says. "We already made our getaway from the Muscle Gang! What was the big idea?"

Remember, we're doing all this talking while sitting in Rocco's upside-down car after an enormous smash-up. And we're thinking this isn't the best idea — you know, in case the car should catch fire and blow up or something like that.

So we start to climb out through the windows.

People on the street are running over to the car, helping us get out and asking if we're all right and everything. It's a mess.

"Yes, thanks! I'm OK. Thank you," I'm saying to all the concerned strangers.

"Just leave me alone, will ya? I'm fine!" Rocco sneers at everyone as he wipes off his pants.

"Yeah, yeah, yeah, yeah! I ain't hurt! Just mind your own business, why don't ya?" Mikey barks at the crowd as he picks up his gun.

Now I can hear a police car siren wailing in the distance. And I feel better and think: That's great! The police are coming to help us.

But Rocco and Mikey don't look so happy about the whole thing.

They give each other a worried glance, then grab me by the shirt collar and start running like mad.

"Come on, kid! We gotta get out of here," Mikey shouts.

"Yeah, what was ya standing there waiting for?" Rocco asks me, puffing as he runs. "Ya know the boss don't want us talking to no cops about nothing."

"B-but we can't just leave the scene of an accident like that, guys," I say. "The car's in the middle of the street. And the cops need us to give them a report or something, don't they?"

"Geez, Babyface! You really must be going loony on us!" Rocco says, pulling me along the sidewalk in a full sprint. "Why should we care what the cops need? Huh?"

We race through several downtown streets, running past the tall buildings and leafy palm trees, then hail a taxi and jump in.

Rocco makes sure I sit in the middle of the back seat, between Mikey and him.

Now I'm getting the feeling that these two brutal mobsters don't trust me.

Hey, what did I do wrong? It's not my fault I can't drive.

But how can I explain to them that I'm really just old Joey from the neighborhood inside a grown-up body? I can't expect them to buy that one.

I hardly believe it myself!

Because even during the gun battle in the car, all these thoughts kept swirling around in back of my head: I'm Babyface the mobster — with Joey the kid's brain! It *can't* be real! But it is! How can this be happening?

So now Rocco gives the cab driver some address in Miami Beach, though I don't recognize the place. Never been there before. And as Rocco and Mikey start talking, I'm not too sure I really want to go there now.

"Yeah, so Mikey — how come you think

Babyface waited so long at the warehouse before making our getaway?" Rocco asks, looking right past me like I'm not even there.

"Yeah, that's a real good question, Rocco. *Real* good question," Mikey says. "Don't make a lot of sense, does it?"

"Nah, it don't," Rocco agrees. "Not for the best getaway driver in the mob, ya know? What do you think, Babyface? Huh?"

And now Rocco is staring right at me, and so is Mikey. And I can feel myself starting to sweat.

A lot.

Chapter Eleven

"You aren't talking about me, are ya guys?" I ask with a nervous smile. "'Cause I know I'm sure not the best getaway driver in the mob. Not old Jo — uh, I mean, not old Babyface!"

"Well, you always was the best — least ways, before today you was, Babyface," Rocco says.

"Yeah, don't you remember after that big bank heist in Fort Lauderdale? You got us out of there even after the joint was surrounded by cops," Mikey says.

I start scratching my head over this one.

I mean, they've got to be wrong about that, ya know? Just an hour ago, I was still Joey, not Babyface. I never drove any getaway car in Fort Lauderdale!

"So me and Mikey was thinking, maybe Babyface don't like us so much no more," Rocco says. "Cause it almost looks like you was working with the Muscle Gang or something, kid!"

"Yeah, we was thinking, maybe Babyface really was trying to get us killed back at the warehouse or maybe after that when he started driving so crazy," Mikey says angrily.

I look back and forth between the two of them, getting sweatier than ever now.

And I try to smile but my lip won't curl the normal way. And I know my goofy grin probably just looks plenty nervous, which it is.

"Me, guys? Nah, not me!" I say with fake confidence. "I'm totally loyal to you guys. I'm in the Killer Mob and that's it for me! I don't need anything from the Muscle Gang, ya know what I mean?"

"Well, we'll just see about that," Mikey says, pointing a threatening finger at me.

"Yeah, we'll just find out if you're a traitor to the Killer Mob or if ya ain't," Rocco says.

I watch in horror as he pulls his gun from a holster under his jacket.

"W-what do, uh, you mean, Rocco?" I stammer.

"I mean, we're taking ya to the boss right now, Babyface! This cab's going to his house in Miami Beach so you can explain the whole thing to him, see?" Rocco says, spitting the words at me. "And if the boss don't like what you tell him — well, all I can say is good luck! I wouldn't want to be in your shoes, after what ya done to us in that getaway car! You're in the worst trouble of your life, kid!"

Chapter Twelve

So we're on the way to the boss's house, see?

But I don't know the boss from any bum in the street — don't know what he looks like, don't know his name, don't know how to act around him, don't know nothing. Uh, I mean, *anything*.

And I'm thinking: This isn't good! Not good at all! Because what happens if I say the wrong thing to the boss? And then maybe he starts to wonder if I really am working for the Muscle Gang! Then old Joey's goose is cooked for sure!

I figure the only way around this mess is to pump the guys for some information about the boss. Maybe I can learn enough so I won't get myself in worse trouble than I'm already in.

"So, uh, Rocco — we're going to the boss's

place, eh?" I ask casually, like I've been there a million times. "Yeah, that's good. It'll be nice to see the joint again. The boss really has a nice dump, doesn't he?"

"How would you know?" Rocco shoots back. "You ain't ever been there in your life, Babyface. I've only been there once before and Mikey ain't ever seen it either. You know that. The boss don't like to do business at home. But in this case, we know he'll want to make an exception, see? After all you done, he's gonna want to talk with you right away."

"Oh, yeah, yeah, sure! I know that!" I lie. "I don't mean it's like I've ever really *seen* the boss's place. But we all hear plenty of things about it. And that's what I mean about it being a nice dump and all. I feel almost like I've seen it before, ya know?"

"You sure are acting strange, kid!" Mikey says, a confused look twisting his eyes and mouth. "If I hadn't seen you today with my own eyes, I wouldn't believe it's really you, Babyface. It's like you're someone else or something."

"Yeah, or maybe you're just drunk on booze or something. Is that it, kid? Have you been drinking again, Babyface?" Rocco asks.

For some reason, Rocco and Mikey erupt into spasms of laughter over this. I don't know what to make of it — so I just keep talking.

"Yeah, sure. Right, Rocco. Ha!" I say with a fake laugh.

Then I start pumping them for info again, hoping to find out more about the boss.

"Like I was saying, the boss really knows how to live, doesn't he? But ya know what I was wondering? No one ever told me what the boss was called before he ran the mob. I mean, did he have another nickname? Or did everyone just use his real name back then?"

And I'm thinking: Maybe at least I can find out what to call this guy when I see him. Because maybe the guys don't call him 'boss' to his face. Who knows?

Rocco and Mikey look like I'm crazy or

something.

"Huh?" Mikey responds.

"What are you talking about, kid?" Rocco inquires with a puzzled expression. "Ya mean, did they ever just call him Bruno? Yeah, right! You know he ain't ever used that name in his life, at least not since he got out of grade school! He hates to be called Bruno! Everyone's just called him 'the boss' since he was about seventeen years old and first joined a gang."

"Yeah, he ain't ever used any other name but that! Except for his wife — Sondra. She's the only person alive who can call him Bruno. And you know that as good as we do," Mikey says suspiciously. "What the heck is wrong with you, Babyface! Why are you asking all these weird questions and all?"

Wow, this is tough. And scary, too!

But I need to find out all I can before meeting the boss —so I keep right on talking.

"Me? Hey, there isn't anything wrong with me, guys!" I laugh nervously. "But I think that little car crash rattled my brains or something. It's like I can't remember anything. So I guess that's why I'm asking all these weird questions, Mikey. Like, for instance, I can't really remember the last time I talked with the boss."

"You oughta remember that, Babyface," Rocco says. "Cause you met him this morning, along with Jackie and Mikey and Jimmy and Lou and me. We all talked about picking up the stolen goods at the warehouse. Ya mean you don't remember that?"

"Yeah, and the boss told you to drive me and Rocco over to the warehouse," Mikey continues. "And that's when the Muscle Gang moved in and tried to blow us away. And you just drove right up with the car and that's when we climbed in, kid. You was doing great to save us — until ya sat there so long, like you was waiting for the Muscle Gang to knock us off or something."

"Oh, sure, sure. This morning!" I reply, like it's all coming back to me now. "Sure, I remember that, right! Yeah, sure I remember meeting with the boss this morning."

Rocco and Mikey look at each other now. They exchange an odd expression, then they both look at me as I slouch between them.

"That's kinda strange that you remember all that, Babyface!" Mikey says.

"Yeah! It's kinda strange all right," Rocco adds. "Cause there *wasn't* no meeting this morning, kid! We just made that up to see what you said. The boss gave us orders two days ago to clear the goods out of that warehouse! And you was in that meeting with Mikey and me. You was right there with us!"

"Yeah and now you're gonna stop lying to us, kid!" Mikey growls, grabbing my shirt and yanking me toward him.

"That's right, kid! The game's up now!" Rocco shouts, holding his large, hairy fist near my nose. "You're gonna tell us the truth, ya hear me? We want to know who you really are! 'Cause one thing is plenty clear now — ya sure ain't Babyface!"

Chapter Thirteen

Uh-oh, I think right away. You'd better come up with something fast here, Joey boy. Or you'll be wearing those cement shoes after all!

So I smile first and then just bust out laughing, ya know? Like it's all a big joke or something. Even though I know the guys aren't joking.

"Ha, ha, ha, ha! Yeah, that's sure a good one, Rocco," I chuckle. "I ain't really Babyface, right? Someone else is just living inside Babyface's body. It's like in the movies, ya know? Like I'm possessed by an evil spirit or something. Yeah, that's it! My head probably will start spinning in circles any minute. Ha, ha, ha, ha!"

But it's not working. Because neither Rocco nor Mikey are laughing — or even cracking a little smile.

Uh-oh again!

"You won't be laughing after ya talk to the boss, kid!" Rocco says. "Ya may not laugh again for a long, long time. If ya know what I mean."

"Yeah. Unless ya can laugh at the bottom of the Miami River," Mikey says.

"I don't know how ya done it, kid! But I know you ain't Babyface! I know that as sure as I'd know my own mother," Rocco says, his fist at my nose again. "You're maybe some look-alike mug who the Muscle Gang found somewhere. Or maybe you're wearing some special mask like they do in the movies to make ya look like our pal. Or maybe you're Babyface's twin brother! But you ain't him. I know it. And Mikey knows it. And pretty soon the boss is gonna know it, too!"

We all get very quiet now as the cab rumbles over the long bridge that leads to Miami Beach. Once we're in the city, we pass flowering tropical bushes and palm trees with clusters of coconuts dangling from them.

Within about five minutes, the cab stops.

We're at the boss's house.

The joint really is like some kind of palace — huge and white, with a large front door painted gold. Rocco rings the doorbell and a maid lets us in and takes us toward some back room.

Inside, the place is kind of surprising. It's decorated pretty junky, really, just a lot of stuff in different colors and everything all tossed together. It almost seems like someone bought a lot of expensive furniture that doesn't really match.

The maid leaves us in a big room, closing the door behind her. This room has a lot of books that look like they've never been opened. And a beautiful large piano that looks like it's never been played. And a long bar that looks like a lot of guys have used it plenty for pouring drinks.

And I'm thinking: Geez, the boss doesn't have very good taste. The house looks real tacky.

So now we're just sitting in this huge room,

Rocco and Mikey and me. And we're not doing or saying anything — just waiting, see?

Waiting for Bruno, who everybody always calls "the boss." Except his wife, who calls him Bruno.

Suddenly, the door bursts open and three guys who look like Rocco and Mikey walk in.

Behind them, strutting slowly, comes the boss.

He's a very tall man — and very fat. His hair is completely white and so is his long mustache. He's smoking a large cigar and carries a small silver gun in a holster around his shoulder.

Rocco and Mikey jump up the minute he enters.

"Hey, boss! Good to see ya," Rocco says with a stiff smile.

"Hi ya, boss! Say, great place ya got here," Mikey says, also trying to smile.

But I can tell both of them are real nervous around this top tough guy. Though they probably aren't as nervous as I am!

"Hi, boss!" I say, smiling as wide as I can spread my lips. "Yeah, great place ya got here! It's just beautiful, ya know?"

Now the three mugs leave the room and I'm alone with Rocco and Mikey. And the boss.

And the boss don't look happy! Uh, I mean, *doesn't* look happy.

"You guys know I hate doing business in my home!" the boss shouts. "Now what the heck is so urgent that ya have to come right over here, huh? That's what I want to know! Why are you guys bothering me?"

"We're real sorry about that, boss," Mikey says timidly.

"Yeah, boss. Sorry. But we know how much ya like Babyface and all," Rocco explains. "And see — well, the kid has done some real strange things today. And Mikey and me, well we was just thinking you'd want to know about it right away."

So Rocco and Mikey tell the whole story to

the boss — about the warehouse and the crazy driving and the weird questions and not remembering anything. They give him all the details, while the boss just watches me as if he were a huge hawk circling over a helpless field mouse.

And I'm starting to sweat again.

"Yeah, so what do you think, boss?" Rocco asks at the end of his tale. "It's almost like Babyface ain't really Babyface, ya know what I mean? What do ya think we ought to do?"

The boss takes a long puff of his cigar and blows the smoke toward my face. I start coughing and hacking from the disgusting smell.

"Well, boys, it's like this, see?" the boss begins, talking very slowly. "What happened today with Babyface has got to make a guy wonder, ya know? It's really got to make a guy wonder if maybe you're right. Maybe this really *isn't* Babyface sitting here!"

"That's right, boss! That's just what we was thinking," Rocco says.

"Yeah, good thinking, boss!" Mikey chimes

in.

"*Shut up!*" the boss hollers at the guys. "Now as I was saying, see? It almost makes a fella wonder if the Muscle Gang has knocked off Babyface somehow — and found someone who looks like him to take over in our mob. What do *you* think about all this, Babyface? Ya been pretty quiet over there."

I gulp hard and try to look as calm as possible. But I can't seem to look calm at all.

My lip starts to tremble a little. I feel just like crying and calling out for my mother.

I want to tell the boss the truth about everything and go home. I want to go back to my old apartment house and my school and my friends.

I want to be just a kid again!

But I'm an adult now. An adult mobster, just like I always thought I wanted to be!

"Boss, this is just crazy! You see my face for yourself," I lie fearfully, tears brimming in my eyes. "How can this be anybody but me? It's Babyface sitting here, boss! You've seen my face a thousand times!"

"Then why was you acting so strange with the boys today? And how's come ya waited so long at the warehouse to get the boys away from the Muscle Gang?" the boss asks, pointing his finger toward me angrily.

"Well, I was, uh . . . that is, I was . . . I mean . . . " I stammer in a panic.

I don't know what to say.

I thought I was smart enough to know my way around, but I need to be smarter!

I thought I was old enough to handle things, but I need to be older!

Still, I've got to try again to come up with some story the boss will believe.

"It was the, uh . . . well, the car was just . . . " I say, a tear starting to stream down my cheek now. Then I break down, pleading for mercy. "Oh boss, you *know* this is me! Why are ya doing this to me? I haven't done anything wrong!"

"Look, boss! Babyface is crying!" Rocco

says.

"Hey, maybe it *is* Babyface after all, huh?" Mikey says. "Ya know, he's the only guy in the mob who cries when he gets all worked up about something. That's why we call him Babyface."

And I'm thinking: Wow! Talk about lucky! It's really good that I'm crying!

Then the boss starts to talk again.

"Yeah, kid! I admit ya look just like Babyface, the best getaway driver in the world," the boss says. "And ya even cry, just like he does sometimes. But I think we should give him the real test, boys! That way, we'll know for sure this really is Babyface — or we'll know if it ain't!"

"What kind of test, boss?" Rocco asks.

"Something no one outside the Killer Mob would know about Babyface! Not even his own sweet mama or nobody," the boss says, staring at me. "What's the only thing you ever drink, Babyface? Just answer me that one question, and we'll know it's you for sure!"

"Hey, great idea, boss! He wouldn't tell no one outside the gang about that," Rocco says.

"Yeah, that's a real good test and all, boss!" Mikey agrees.

"W-what's the only, uh, thing I like to drink?" I ask, feeling sick to my stomach. "You mean, like anything at all, boss? Is that what you mean?"

"Yeah, that's right, kid," the boss says. "The real Babyface will only touch one thing, whether he's at home alone or out at bars with the boys. If you're really Babyface, like ya say, you know what that is. And if ya know what's good for your health, kid, you'd better give me the right answer! *Right now!*"

Chapter Fourteen

I'm really trapped this time, I think. I'm done for and nothing can save me!

I'm sweating like a pig and squirming in my seat and trying like crazy to smile, with the boss all the time staring straight in my eyes.

Rocco and Mikey are watching real close too. I almost think they want me to give the wrong answer so they can toss me in the river or something.

What would Babyface drink, what would Babyface drink, what would Babyface drink? I keep asking myself that question over and over.

And I have absolutely no idea.

If he's a mobster, he may drink nothing but alcohol! It seems like all mobsters drink a lot of alcohol, even though it's really bad for you.

Then, as I look at Rocco and Mikey, something comes to me. Yeah, sure — I remember when Rocco made a joke about Babyface drinking alcohol.

He said something to me like, "Maybe you was drunk," or words kind of like that. And it was all a big joke to Mikey and Rocco, and they laughed so hard I thought they was going explode.

So maybe that's my tip-off, I'm figuring. Maybe Babyface doesn't like any alcohol at all. And if he doesn't, maybe his favorite drink is just the same as my favorite drink.

I decide this is the only chance I have and, besides, the boss is waiting for the answer and I have to say something now.

So I kind of offer a silent prayer and hold my breath and then I just blurt it out.

"Root beer!" I answer, closing my eyes as a frightened tear rolls down my cheek.

Rocco and Mikey look over at the boss, waiting for his reaction.

The boss sits quietly a moment, still staring at

me.

Then he smiles.

"Yeah, all right, kid! You're Babyface for sure," the boss says with a laugh. "It always cracks me up how you get so embarrassed about drinking nothing but root beer. I love the way you make bartenders pretend they're really pouring beer in your glass. Ha! And I know you ain't never told no one that you started drinking root beer when you was twenty-years-old — so you've got to be Babyface after all."

"Sure I'm Babyface, boss! You *know* I am!" I say, more relieved than I've ever felt in my life. "I was just having a bad day, boss! I'm sorry about the slow getaway at the warehouse and driving nutty and all. Just a real bad day. Won't let it happen again!"

"You'd *better* not let it happen again, kid!" the boss snarls. "Cause if it does, no amount of root beer can save ya. I'll know for sure that you're in with the Muscle Gang and you'll be a goner for sure, see?"

You'd better believe I see! I know just what the boss means!

I'm learning about the mob real fast — faster than I ever really wanted to learn.

I'm finding out that you have to do exactly what these gangsters want you to do every minute.

Or else!

And I'm thinking: This could be a big problem. I don't like this mob business as much as I thought I would. What am I going to have to do for The Killer Mob? I sure don't want to hurt anybody or steal nothing from nobody.

Uh, I mean, *anything from anybody.*

But now the boss is saying he has some job to keep me busy this afternoon. And right away I know it's not anything I want to do, not anymore than I want to beat up people or steal stuff.

Really, it's something I *can't* do.

Because the boss is telling me I have to drive again.

I have to take *the boss's car* this time — and

I have to drive *the boss's wife* around Miami Beach!

Me! Old Joey, the thirteen-year-old who's living inside Babyface the mobster's body!

Me! Joey, who can't drive! And now I'll be driving around the wife of the boss of the Killer Mob!

"And if you're a smart kid like I've always thought, you won't have any accidents this time, Babyface," the boss says sternly.

What can I say? I have to smile, just as if I really was the great getaway driver he thinks I am.

"Uh, yeah, r-right! S-sure, boss!" I answer. "Whatever you want!"

"You won't go around speeding or driving crazy or nothing. You'll drive real slow and careful and safe-like with my wife, right?" the boss says. "In fact, you better be the safest driver on the road this afternoon, Babyface! *Got it*? Now go pull the car up to the front of the house. My wife wants to go shopping and she'll be down any minute."

Chapter Fifteen

Now I'm really swimming in hot soup, ya know?

If I put one little dent in the boss's car, or one little scratch on the boss's wife, my life isn't worth a nickel.

But what choice do I got? Uh, I mean, *have*.

I'm really nervous now and I'm walking to the car thinking: Maybe I should run for it while I have a chance. I might get a block or two away before the boss knows I'm gone.

But, no, I'm too smart for that, see? Because then the boss will only think I'm in the Muscle Gang for sure. And he'll send out guys all over Miami searching for me, looking to rub me out.

And they'll find me too, sooner or later. You

can be sure of that, pal!

So I figure my best shot is to get inside the boss's car and try to drive like I've seen my dad drive so many times. Only I wish I'd paid more attention.

I'm in the garage now and I see the boss owns a real beauty of a car — a 1936 Rolls Royce, all silver and gleaming like it was brand new. Wow!

This baby must be worth a fortune, I think. Great! That means it'll cost a fortune to fix if I smash it up.

I sit inside on the gray leather seats. Then I remember to turn the key, real gentle, and the engine begins to purr like a kitten. And I think back to what Dad does when he backs up from the apartment house driveway — he always turns around to face the rear and goes real, real slow.

So that's what I try to do. *Go real, real slow*!

And so far it's working pretty good, ya know? I haven't run over his lawn or hit a bush or a tree or anything yet.

I back up the car straight as an arrow and

then I just sit there, waiting nervously for the boss's wife to come out. I know that's when the hard part will really begin.

Because then I've got to actually steer this huge boat of a car around corners and through traffic and all. It won't be easy, but I've got no other choice, do I?

I see the front door open and this beautiful lady walks out.

She has flowing red hair that falls around her shoulders, and long pretty legs and she's wearing high heels and a nice green dress. And she has a nice face and smiles a beautiful, kind smile as she walks up to the car.

I get out of the car and open her door and she thanks me really politely. What a nice lady! She doesn't seem like the kind of woman who would marry a mob boss, ya know what I mean?

And now it's time to put the car in gear again and back out of the driveway and head toward the stores of Miami Beach, wherever they are.

So I move out into the street, real slow, just like when I backed the car out of the garage. And for a few seconds I think: Maybe this won't be so tough after all.

But in the rear-view mirror I see the boss's wife looking upset.

"What are you doing?" she asks me. "You're driving on the wrong side of the road, Babyface!"

"Oh! Uh, yeah, right, ma'am!" I reply, getting rattled now. "I, uh, well — ya see, well, I'm sorry about that."

No matter how hard I try, I just can't seem to steer the car straight. It wobbles from one lane of the street to the other. Luckily, we're still on small roads in an area of houses and apartments, with no traffic.

But now I see we're approaching a big intersection only a few blocks ahead. And I remember what happened the *last* time I drove into a major intersection.

Pow! The car smash-up of the century!

"Babyface, what's wrong with you today?"

the boss's wife says, her voice worried. "Look out! You almost ran over that curb and up on to the sidewalk!"

"I'm really sorry, ma'am! I'm not quite myself somehow, I think," I say feebly.

I know I'm in plenty of trouble now. I still have no idea how to drive a car — and I can't hide it from the boss's wife any longer.

In the rear-view mirror, I can see her watching me, like she's thinking about something real hard — you know, trying to figure something out.

"Babyface, pull the car over and stop! Right now!" she orders me. "Stop the car before you kill us both!"

So I steer over toward the right as best I can and actually bump the tires into the curb. And then I stop the car and turn around to face the boss's wife. I just know she's going to phone her husband and probably have me killed or something.

"Move over, Babyface," she says. "I'm coming up there to drive."

And that's what the boss's wife does — she gets in the driver's seat and then pulls into the big intersection and off down the road, heading for her favorite stores.

"What's your real name?" she asks suddenly.

And I'm really startled by this, see? And really scared!

"Huh? What do you m-mean, ma'am? My name's B-B-Babyface!" I stutter.

She just smiles, a very kind and very pretty smile.

"No, it isn't. I know better than that," she purrs quietly, her voice barely louder than the gentle sound of the car engine. "I know you're someone else — another person in Babyface's body. I know you're really just a teenager and you've never learned to drive a car. And I know just how you got where you are now — and I also know why."

I'm so shocked by all this that I can't even try to deny it. It's the truth — but how can she possibly know that?

"B-but I don't get it, ma'am," I say. "If you know that much about me, how come you're not driving me back to your husband so you can tell him about it? And then Rocco and Mikey can knock me off or something, huh?"

"There's a very simple reason. Actually, two reasons," the boss's wife answers with a smile. "First, because no one would believe me. And second, because I'm just a teenager from the neighborhood, too. I'm just like you, a kid stuck inside some adult's body. And, unfortunately, we're both trapped here now, forced to live with a bunch of killer thugs forever!"

Chapter Sixteen

"*What?*" I shout. "Are you *serious?*"

"Perfectly," the boss's wife answers. "I'm a Miami kid from Southwest Eighth Street, probably just like you."

"That's a good guess," I said. "But really my parents live in an apartment house on Southwest Twelfth Avenue, just north of Southwest Eighth Street."

"Just around the corner from my mother's home," she says. "I felt sure you were from the same neighborhood as I am. I could just tell."

But now I start getting a little suspicious — how does this lady know so much anyway? And if she's really just another kid like me, how come she can talk so good and knows how to drive and all?

Maybe the boss is trying to trick me somehow so he can find out the truth, then have the boys rub me out! Hey, is this a set-up or what?

"If you're really a kid, why do you know how to drive this car and I don't?" I ask her directly. "It doesn't make sense."

"When I first got to be part of the mob, I couldn't drive anymore than you can. I couldn't do a lot of things most adults know how to do," she replied. "But I've had to learn some things. I've been Bruno's wife for nearly three years now. I've taught myself how to drive and I've studied and learned many things by taking classes, including how to speak proper English. I don't care how those thugs talk! I decided that if I'm going to be an adult, I may as well learn the most basic things an adult should know."

"But this is *crazy*!" I cry. "Stuff like this just doesn't happen in real life. I feel like I'm a character in a book or something! It's like science fiction. How did we get here anyway?"

"I don't really understand all the details yet. But I have figured out the main points, I think," she explains, maneuvering the Rolls Royce expertly through the crowded streets of Miami Beach. "You see, I was a kid who hated being a kid. More than anything else in the world, I wanted to grow up. And because I lived around all the gangsters in our neighborhood, I grew up wanting to be just like them. I thought if I could just marry the boss of the Killer Mob, I'd be happier than any person on earth."

"Yeah, I know what you mean," I say. "It was kind of like that with me, too. I wanted to be a mobster real bad — ya know, join up with the Killer Mob boys and all."

"Yes, that's what I thought. And what happened is that, somehow, we simply got our wish. We became just what we had always wanted to be," she says.

She swerves in and out of traffic, just as smooth as silk.

"One day I was a thirteen-year-old girl named

Patty, riding my bicycle along the street and hating my life," she says. "I was trying to follow the car of the Killer Mob's boss when I fell off my bike and bumped my head hard on the road. When I woke up, I was suddenly Sondra, the mob boss's wife! I had taken over her body somehow, but I still had Patty's teenage mind."

"Wow! That's wild, isn't it? It's just like me," I say in amazement. "Sondra, huh? Say, that's a nice name. But I like Patty, too. My real name's Joey. Pleased to meet ya!"

"Right now, I'd give anything if I could return to being a thirteen-year-old named Patty in my parents' neighborhood," Sondra says sadly. "I hate living with gangsters. They're rude and stupid and mean and violent. I can't imagine why I ever wanted to be like them."

"Yeah, me neither," I say. "Uh, I mean, *I can't either*. But excuse me, Patty . . . "

"You'd better call me Sondra. And I'll just call you Babyface," she interrupts. "That way we won't mistakenly use our old names around the mobsters, and make them suspicious."

"Yeah, right. Good idea," I say. "But Sondra, how did you ever figure I wasn't really Babyface. I don't get it."

"It all added up. First, you couldn't drive, and Babyface was an excellent driver," she says. "Also, you called me ma'am, and Babyface was never that polite. There were other clues, too. After all that, I simply guessed that the same terrible thing that happened to me also had happened to you."

"It's a terrible mess, isn't it?" I say, tears suddenly brimming in my eyes. "What are we gonna do? I don't have a clue, ya know?"

"Yes, I know. I've been in this mess for a long time and I haven't a clue either, Babyface," Sondra sighs. "I didn't like childhood because it seemed so unfair. Everyone could tell me what to do simply because they were adults. I was smart for my age and wanted to make up my own mind about things. But now more than anything I just want to be a kid again!"

"How come, Sondra?" I ask. "Just 'cause of living with the mob and all, ya mean?"

"That's part of it, certainly," she says. "But, also, being an adult carries with it so many responsibilities. You have to learn things and understand things and cope with things children never have to even think about. All of that is fine — as long as you grow up learning and understanding along the way. By the time you finally reach adulthood, you're ready to handle it all."

"Yeah, I kind of get what ya mean, Sondra," I say. "You mean that because we're just kids in big bodies, we're not really ready to be adults yet."

"Exactly, Babyface. That's what I mean," Sondra says. "We haven't learned to understand other people the way most adults know how to understand them. Or how to control our emotions the way adults must control them. Or how to do things as simple as driving a car or applying for a credit card or balancing a check book. Adults deal with a lot of complicated problems and worries. We're just not prepared for that at thirteen years old."

"Yeah, so I guess maybe we should have tried to be happier when we was kids, huh? Uh, I mean, when we *were* kids," I say. "I guess we should have just enjoyed stuff while we were young and let ourselves grow up naturally, right?"

"Yes, that's what I believe, Babyface. But it's too late for that now," Sondra says. "We'd better worry about a more immediate problem. We have to think up some way to make you look very ill tonight. You have to look so ill that you can't drive or hold a gun — or even leave our house."

"Huh? I mean, excuse me, Sondra? I don't understand what you're talking about," I say, scratching my head nervously.

"What I'm talking about is the big job Bruno has planned for tonight. You don't even know about it yet, do you?" Sondra says.

"No! What big job?" I ask, getting real worried again.

"I'm afraid Bruno plans to order a carload of his thugs to attack the Muscle Gang at their head-quarters tonight," she says. "He told me that it'll be a nasty gunfight. Bruno says most of the men he picks to go will never come back alive."

She stops and looks over at me, with worry in her eyes.

"And the worst part of it is," she says, "he expects you to lead the attack!"

Chapter Seventeen

"*Me? Lead the attack!*" I shout, almost jumping out of my seat. "Why *me*? I'm just Babyface, the getaway driver!"

"He told me you were the world's best getaway driver — and that you could also handle a machine gun with the best of them," Sondra says. "Bruno said that if the Killer Mob is ever going to wipe out the Muscle Gang, he has to put all his best men in that car tonight and let them fight it out. And so he wants you to drive the car right through the front window of their headquarters, just smash right in. Then you're supposed to jump out of the car and blast away with your machine gun."

Getaway driver? Machine gun? No way, not old Joey!

"Geez, Sondra! I can't do something like that," I say, my lip trembling with fear. "But how am I gonna get out of it? The boss will never believe me if I pretend to be sick."

"I don't know what else to do, Babyface," she says. "That's the only idea I've come up with so far. But you're right. It may not be enough to convince Bruno."

"Maybe I ought to just run away to South America or somewhere while I have the chance, huh?" I say. "Maybe you could drop me at the airport and give me some money or something. All I know is I can't go through with that attack tonight. Even if I could drive, I can't shoot a gun. And I wouldn't want to shoot a gun even if I knew how to do it!"

"I know, Babyface. I know," Sondra says sympathetically. "I wish there were an easy answer. When you're a kid it often seems like there's one easy answer to everything, doesn't it?"

"Yeah, I . . . I guess so," I say, kind of puzzled.

"You know, like when we were children living in the neighborhood. All we wanted was to grow up and be around the mob, and then everything would be great," Sondra says. "But now we know that it isn't great. As an adult, I've learned that there aren't always easy solutions to problems. But usually there are *good* solutions, if you look for them hard enough."

Sondra is still driving the Rolls Royce through the Miami Beach streets, down Ocean Boulevard beside the beach and the sidewalk restaurants and all. And I'm thinking about the stuff she just said, not really getting all of it right away, ya know?

I mean, what is she saying anyway? I just know that I *need* an easy answer, and I need it real fast.

In only a few hours, the boss is going to send me on some big mission to wipe out the Muscle Gang. A suicide mission!

But right then, as Sondra eases the Rolls

Royce around a corner, something really strange starts to happen.

For a minute, I'm not sure what's going on.

A big black car squeals out of an alley and blocks the road so we can't go forward, see? And then another big black car screeches around the corner from behind and keeps us from backing up.

"Aaaaagggh!" Sondra screams, looking terrified.

It's pretty clear that Sondra understands what's happening — and I know that whatever it is, it's not good! But for another few seconds I'm still not figuring it out myself.

Then a bunch of big tough guys climb out of the two cars and head toward us, and now I get it, all right. At least I know that I won't be going on any attack of the Muscle Gang headquarters tonight.

Because these guys in the black cars *are* the Muscle Gang.

A bunch of thugs from the rival mob are kidnapping the boss's wife and me! Me — the guy they believe is Babyface, the Killer Mob's best getaway driver!

Our car is totally surrounded by the Muscle Gang!

And there's nothing we can do to stop this gang of hoods from taking us prisoner!

Chapter Eighteen

Geez!

This mobster life isn't like I thought it would be!

These guys really are tough and bad, just like Sondra said.

And they're always trying to hurt each other for some reason.

So I'm thinking to myself: This isn't any game now, Joey old boy! The Muscle Gang's got ya and you're done for this time!

We're still in the car, waiting to see if the Muscle Gang is going to rub us out or what. I have tears rolling down my cheeks and I'm huddling real close to Sondra, as if she's my mother or something.

I just want to go home!

The thugs are pointing guns at us now and telling us to get out if we know what's good for our health. So we do exactly what they want.

And pretty soon, Sondra and I are inside one of those big black cars — sitting between two hairy thugs who sure ain't smiling at us. Uh, I mean, *aren't* smiling at us.

"So you're the great, big getaway driver for the Killer Mob, huh?" one thug says to me. "You just look like a scared little punk to me. Crying like a baby and all! At least now I know why they call ya Babyface."

"Leave him alone," Sondra says sharply. "I don't know why you're bothering us. We can't tell you anything. Babyface was just taking me on a shopping trip."

"Yeah, sister — we knew where ya was going," the second thug says to her. "We was following you two all over the city. And now we're taking ya to meet someone. Ain't we, Al?"

"Yeah, that's right," says Al, the first thug.

"We're taking ya both to meet someone. But we don't think you're gonna like making his acquaintance, if ya know what I mean! Ha, ha, ha, ha!"

The two big jerks start laughing like hyenas or something. Yeah, right — big joke!

Maybe twenty minutes later, the car pulls up in front of a big white mansion that looks a lot like the house Sondra and the boss own. It's another palace with a huge wooden door, only this door is painted silver instead of gold.

When we get inside, all the furniture and everything looks just as mismatched and tacky as the stuff in the boss's place.

Geez! Mobsters!

Are they all a bunch of dopes or what?

So we're waiting in a room in some other mobster's house, another ugly room with a big bar and a lot of books no one ever opens and a nice piano no one ever plays. And then a large door opens and three tough guys walk in, one of them carrying a briefcase. And they're followed by a fat man with white hair who's wearing a gray suit.

He almost looks like the boss of the Killer Mob, but he isn't.

"Don't get up, you two," the fat man says, standing beside a large window. "We got some talkin' to do and ya might as well stay sittin' down. I don't like to waste time, ya know? My name's Tony. I'm the boss of the Muscle Gang. Maybe ya heard of me? Ha, ha, ha, ha!"

And now Tony, the fat mob boss, starts laughing, and the three mugs with him laugh as hard as they can.

"Yes, we've heard of you, Tony. But I want to know what we're doing here," Sondra says bravely. "I'm not in the Killer Mob. And Babyface is just a chauffeur, a professional driver. Nothing more than that. We can't tell you anything."

"Not so fast, little lady," Tony snaps at her. "I think ya can tell us plenty, if ya want to. And ya'd better want to, see? Say, you're even better lookin' than the boys told me. That Bruno done all right for himself."

"Never mind that! Leave her alone," I shoot back. "What do you want from us, Tony? We don't know anything that could help you."

"Well, see now, that's not what I hear from my friends, kid!" Tony says angrily. "Cause what I hear is that the Killer Mob is plannin' a big hit on our gang sometime soon. I got friends everywhere, kid — even inside the Killer Mob. But what we don't know is *where* your mob is gonna attack us. And we still don't know *when* either, ya see? And so that's what you two is gonna tell us. *Ya got it?*"

"We don't know that, you fool!" Sondra lies. "I'm just Bruno's wife. Why would he tell me? We don't talk about his business. And he certainly wouldn't tell his driver until just before the attack. Babyface doesn't know anything."

Tony sits down beside Sondra now, staring suspiciously into her eyes. He doesn't say a word for a long time.

"Ya know what, lady? I don't believe ya!" he

hollers suddenly. "And I don't have a lot of patience either! So one of you better tell me where and when the Killer Mob is going to hit us! And ya better do it right now!"

"And what if we don't?" Sondra asks defiantly.

"If ya don't? Ha! Hey boys, she wants to know what will happen if they don't talk!" Tony laughs to his three thugs. Then he looks at us both and snarls. "If ya don't lady, I'm gonna have the boys take Babyface outside and strap a bomb to his back and stick him in the trunk of that black car. And then they'll push a button and blow the bomb and the car — and Babyface — to smithereens!"

Chapter Nineteen

No, no, no, I'm thinking to myself. Just when I thought it couldn't get any worse for me, it gets worse for me!

It was bad enough just turning into Babyface the mobster. Especially when I turned into a getaway driver who can't drive.

But then the Muscle Gang took me hostage. And now their boss wants to blow me up!

"M-maybe we'd, uh, b-better tell him what he wants to know, S-Sondra," I stammer.

"Yeah, that's right, kid. Now you're gettin' smart, ya see?" Tony says. "But don't take too long to get smarter! 'Cause we got everything ready for ya, just in case."

The thug with the briefcase opens it up. And

he pulls out this huge red bomb and holds it proudly in the air, like he's just won some kind of bowling trophy or whatever. Geez!

This mug with the bomb is actually smiling.

And now I can tell that Sondra understands Tony is serious and all. And she's ready to spill the beans in order to save my life.

"All right, Tony. You win," she says softly. "I do have a little information and I'll be happy to tell you everything I know. It's not as if I really love Bruno or anyone in the Killer Mob, anyway."

"Now you're talkin', sister. Let's have the info," Tony says.

I'm feeling plenty relieved because it looks like I've escaped one more brush with death, another very close call.

But then I notice something strange out of the corner of my eye — and I start worrying again.

Because through the large window, I see someone crawling around in the bushes outside. Then I see *two* someones crawling around outside. Then *three*, then *four*!

There's something very weird going on here — and I'm sure it's going to be dangerous.

Then two of these guys peek carefully inside the house, looking at me through the window while Tony and his boys are busy watching Sondra.

I can see that the guys outside are Jackie and Rocco from the Killer Mob. Here, at the home of the Muscle Gang's boss!

They hold their fingers to their lips, telling me to be quiet.

Shhhhh!

That's when I know the boss of the Killer Mob has found out that Sondra and I have been kidnapped — and he's gotten mad and decided to attack the Muscle Gang earlier than planned!

In a matter of minutes, there's going to be a huge war between the Killer Mob and the Muscle Gang!

Guns will be flashing! Bullets will fly everywhere!

And me?

Yeah, you know it, pal — I'll be sitting right in the middle of the whole mess!

Chapter Twenty

Oh, no!

Sondra! She's in real danger, too!

And she's been really kind to me.

I have to help her! I've got to do something to let her know she's in danger!

So I sit looking at her and when she finally glances back at me, I roll my eyes toward the window — ya know, trying to make her look that direction. And that's when Sondra notices Jackie and Rocco, too.

And now she starts acting really nervous because she understands what's happening. And what's about to happen.

"Uh, well, all I really know is that my husband said his men planned to attack your gang to-

Sondra says very slowly, looking around the room. And I know she's looking for some place to hide when the gunplay starts. "So you see, uh, Tony. . ."

"Stop stalling, sister!" Tony yells angrily. "Give me the lowdown, ya see? If ya know the hit is gonna be tonight, ya must know where. Say, you're acting pretty strange all of a sudden, lady. What are ya looking around the room for, anyway?"

With those words, we hear an enormous explosion at the front of the house!

It sounds like a car blew up outside or something!

Suddenly, machine gun fire pours down on Tony's house like rain from a hurricane!

From all sides at once, machine guns blast away furiously!

Five guys run down the hall and burst into the room, mugs from the Muscle Gang coming with news for their boss.

"Tony, it's the Killer Mob!" one of them

shouts. "They're all over the place! Looks like they've got us surrounded!"

Tony turns to face Sondra, clenching his teeth fiercely.

"So the hit is gonna be tonight, huh? I should have known I couldn't trust ya!" he yells, pulling a gun from under his suit jacket. "I should rub ya out for lying to me like that, lady!"

"Come on, Tony! There's no time for that now!" another of his mugs shouts. "We've got to get ya out of this room and put ya somewhere safe! The Killer Mob's everywhere!"

The five guys grab Tony and hustle him out of the room, while the other three thugs from the Muscle Gang stay behind, firing away with their guns.

It's getting really crazy now!

The Killer Mob hammers the house with everything it's got. Bullets smash through windows and slam into the piano and book case.

The guys outside run around all over the

...s they attack the house, shooting while they sprint among the trees and bushes.

Inside, all the Muscle Gang's guys race around like mad, rushing to this room or that so they can defend their boss's house.

I duck down on the floor. Slowly and carefully, I creep toward Sondra. She's also lying on the floor, trembling with terror at the barrage of bullets.

"Come on! Follow me," I shout over the awful noise.

Together, we crawl along the floor toward the heavy wooden bar. We crouch behind it. This seems like the safest place to be right now.

We hear gunfire all around us.

Pistols and rifles: *Kaaa-paaap! Kaaa-paaap! Kaaa-paaap!*

Machine guns: *Rrraackeeettaa! Rrraackeeettaa! Rrraackeeettaa!*

"W-we'll be OK here I think, Sondra," I say. "Let's just hide behind this bar until the shooting stops."

"We'd better hope the Killer Mob wins this battle, Babyface!" Sondra says, her voice quivering with fear. "If the Muscle Gang wins, Tony and his boys will do both of us in for sure! He thinks I was lying to him!"

I know she's right and I start to worry about that very thing while the guns keep firing.

Kaaa-paaap! Kaaa-paaap! Kaaa-paaap!

Rrraackeeettaa! Rrraackeeettaa!

Rrraackeeettaa!

Finally it looks like the Killer Mob is going to win the gunfight, after all. Except I'm not too sure we'll be alive to see their victory!

Because, as more guys from our mob surround the house, the gunfire gets heavier and heavier. Bullets crash into everything! Glass flies all over the room!

Sondra and I lay flat on the floor, hands over our ears to keep out the terrible racket from the guns.

Kaaa-paaap! Kaaa-paaap! Kaaa-paaap!

Rrraackeeettaa! Rrraackeeettaa!
Rrraackeeettaa!

Someone from the Killer Mob tosses a smoke canister inside the house, which spreads a dense white cloud throughout the room.

That makes things even scarier because bullets are still zipping all around — but now no one can see their hand in front of their face.

The three thugs from the Muscle Gang turn and run from the room like scared rabbits.

"We'd better get out of here, too!" I shout to Sondra.

So we leap to our feet and run for the door as fast as we can.

But with all the smoke, we still can't see anything!

We stumble into the book case. Then we bump into the piano.

Where's the door?

Some guys from the Killer Mob come storming through the large broken window behind us like soldiers landing on a beach, firing away with their machine guns! They're inside the house.

At that exact moment, a bunch of guys from the Muscle Gang come running back into the room through the door in front of us, firing away with *their* machine guns!

Heavy smoke hangs everywhere. Nobody can see what they're shooting at.

Mobsters behind us!

Gangsters in front of us!

And Sondra and I are trapped in the middle!

From the back or from the front, one of the thugs is sure to nail us with his bullets!

I realize Sondra and I haven't got one chance in a million. It's totally hopeless!

The only thing I can think to do is scream at all of these jerks who are shooting their guns.

"Stop it! Stop it! Stop it!" I shout at the top of my lungs, standing in a roomful of gunfire and smoke.

"You're all crazy! I don't want to join any mob! *I just want to be a kid again! Stop shooting at us! Stop all this shooting! Please everyone, stop shooting!*"

Chapter Twenty-One

"Son? Are you OK?" a woman's voice is saying to me. "Shhhh, shhhh. Stop screaming, son. It's all right. Are you OK, kid?"

"Huh? Uh, what . . . " I say. My head feels groggy and sore. "W-what's happening?"

I look around and I see policemen and policewomen everywhere.

Blue lights are flashing from the top of police cars and TV cameras are rolling and it's really strange, like a scene from a movie or something.

"Are you all right, son?" a police officer says. She's looking down at me with a beautiful, kind smile. And I notice she has long red hair, and looks a little like Sondra. "You took quite a hit on the head, kid. You were knocked unconscious. Are you OK

117

now?"

"Uh, w-what? A hit on the head? Knocked, uh, unconscious?" I say, still not sure what's going on. But I see that I'm lying in the street near the warehouse, right where I fell on that oil spot, remember?

"I don't get it, officer," I say. "What happened to me?"

"Well, what happened is that you're a hero, son!" the officer says with a big smile. "You helped us capture some of the worst gangsters in Miami!"

"I did?" I ask. "How did I do that?"

"Well, from what we can tell, you were kidnapped by some members of the Killer Mob. Is that right?" the policewoman asks.

"Yes, that's true," I respond, sitting up slowly. "They were angry because I threatened to rat on them to the Muscle Gang."

"Well, it seems that after the Killer Mob boys brought you to their warehouse, the Muscle Gang found you there and started to attack. Do you remember that?" the officer wonders.

"Yes, ma'am," I answer. "I was caught right in the middle. The Muscle Gang was shooting at me from the front. The Killer Mob was shooting at me from behind. Then I just ran!"

"That was smart, son. You got out of the way and let those two terrible gangs fight it out among themselves," the policewoman says.

"How did you catch them anyway?" I say.

"Some businessmen from other warehouses in this area reported a gun battle and we sent a huge squad of police cars over there. We caught several gang members as they were shooting at each other," she says. "But if you hadn't threatened the Killer Mob to begin with, they never would have kidnapped you. And none of this would have happened."

"I hope you arrested them all!" I say.

"You bet we did, son. All of them," the policewoman says. "Plus, we arrested the Killer Mob's boss for running an organization involved with kidnapping. And we arrested the Muscle Gang's boss for running an organization that began a gun battle on city streets. And now the FBI is beginning a big investigation into both gangs. These mobs probably won't cause any more trouble for a long time!"

"That's great! I hate mobsters!" I say, rubbing my head. "Ouch! It really hurts! So was I just lying here during this whole gun fight? You mean I was only dreaming everything else — about the getaway car and the attack on Tony's house and all? It just seemed so — so real!"

"Well, I only know you banged your head hard on the street, son. And while I was trying to help you, you started to shout things like, 'I just want to be a kid again. Stop shooting at us,' " the officer says. "So yes, I guess maybe after you were hurt you had some kind of dream about the mob."

It's really hard for me to believe!

It was all just a weird, awful dream? I never really turned into Babyface the mobster?

I was just Joey the kid all that time?

Wow!

So now the pretty officer with the long red hair helps me stand up and walks me to a police car. A whole bunch of TV and newspaper reporters and photographers gather around me.

They're asking me questions and I'm trying to answer, even though the bump on my head still aches pretty bad.

I tell them the truth.

I tell them how badly I wanted to be a mobster.

And I tell them how I hated being just a thirteen-year-old kid.

But I also tell them that I don't want to be a mobster anymore — and that I don't even want to talk like mobsters, either.

And I also tell them that I'm not in quite as big a rush to grow up as I used to be.

"I don't know exactly what happened to me after I fell on the street and hit my head," I say to the reporters. "But somehow I understand better now that I have plenty of things to learn before I become an adult. And maybe I ain't as smart as I thought I was. Uh, I mean, maybe I'm *not* as smart as I thought I was. Because it's sure not very smart to hang around terrible guys who carry guns and shoot at each other and talk like stupid jerks!"

"Do you have any advice for kids your own age, Joey?" one reporter asks.

"Sure, I do. I'd tell them to learn everything they can while they're still young," I reply. "And I'd tell them to just relax and enjoy things, too! Don't worry so much about small stuff, like adults who boss you around sometimes. Because it won't be long before you're a grown-up just like them. And then you'll have plenty of important things to worry about, like how to be a good driver and balancing your checkbook and everything."

The policewoman drives me home, and I'm really glad I don't have to think about driving any car myself for a few years.

I feel happier to see my parents and our little apartment house than I've ever felt before.

And I smile all through dinner and it feels really good to be safe in my own home again.

Hey Joey — you know what? Maybe you *aren't* as smart as you thought you were, I'm thinking to myself during dinner. But you know what else? You're only thirteen years old. And maybe you're getting a little smarter all the time.

And you know what else?

I hate to admit it, but it's true, I think.

Maybe — yeah, just maybe — it's pretty good to be a kid after all!

LET, LET, LET THE MAILMAN GIVE YOU COLD, CLAMMY *SHIVERS! SHIVERS! SHIVERS!!!*

A Frightening Offer: Buy the first *Shivers* book at $3.99 and pick each additional book for only $1.99. Please include $2.00 for shipping and handling. Canadian orders: Please add $1.00 per book. (Allow 4-6 weeks for delivery.)

__ #1 The Enchanted Attic
__ #2 A Ghastly Shade of Green
__ #3 Ghost Writer
__ #4 The Animal Rebellion
__ #5 The Locked Room
__ #6 The Haunting House
__ #7 The Awful Apple Orchard
__ #8 Terror on Troll Mountain
__ #9 The Mystic's Spell
__ #10 The Curse of the New Kid
__ #11 Guess Who's Coming For Dinner?
__ #12 The Secret of Fern Island
__ #13 The Spider Kingdom

__ #14 The Curse in the Jungle
__ #15 Pool Ghoul
__ #16 The Beast Beneath the Boardwalk
__ #17 The Ghosts of Camp Massacre
__ #18 Your Momma's a Werewolf
__ #19 The Thing in Room 601
__ #20 Babyface and the Killer Mob
__ #21 A Waking Nightmare
__ #22 Lost in Dreamland
__ #23 Night of the Goat Boy
__ #24 Ghosts of Devil's Marsh

I'm scared, but please send me the books checked above.

$_____ is enclosed.

Name_____

Address_____

City_____ State_____ Zip _____

Payment only in U.S. Funds. Please no cash or C.O.D.s.
Send to: Paradise Press, 8551 Sunrise Blvd. #302, Plantation, FL 33322.